from
JIM AND
LOUISE

Have a Good Roam

A storybook song

Joan Gold Cypress

illustrations by
Barbara Counsil

Roam on over to the end of the story to
download *Have a Good Roam* music and
trim out your lyric poster. Both are FREE!

Have a Good Roam

Copyright ©2022 by Joan Gold Cypress

Printed in the United States of America

Contributors
Troy Cypress Broadnax: *Vocals, Music*
Dawn Cypress Broadnax: *Vocals, Drums*
Gus Russell: *Keyboard*
Paul Biondi: *Flute, Saxophone*
Jennifer Andrews: *Cover Design*

Queen Scarlett Productions
2251 W. 29th Avenue
Eugene, OR 97405
queenscarlettproductions.com

ISBN: 978-1-7323036-2-1

To mom, Shirley Silverfield Gold,
with gratitude for her guidance
to shoot for the stars.

Needlepoint picture by Shirley

Over the rainbow,
where some gather round

You search for true love,

will it be found?

After a brainstorm,
you'll master the dream

Gather your courage
and have a good roam

Some days are sunny, happy and bright

Some days are gloomy,
as dark as the night.

It's only weather,
a change will come through

Keep your chin up,
that's what we gotta do.

Over the rainbow,

where some gather round

You search for true love, will it be found?

Follow
Your heart

And know that life's not what it may seem.

The road can narrow be bumpy or wide

Surrender along no matter which side.

Look for the magic,
see where it goes

Stay focused, the sign ahead shows.

The sky's the limit, the stars will guide you

Just relax and enjoy the view.

Share with your neighbor
and always be kind

Reach out, look up
and see what you'll find.

Over the rainbow, where some gather round.

You search for true love,

will it be found?

After a brainstorm,
you'll master the dream

And know that life's not
what it may seem.

Gather your courage
and have a good roam

Just remember, there's no place like home.

Have a good roam,
There's no place like home...

Have a good roam,
There's no place like home...

Have a good roam...

Turn the page for your
FREE Have a Good Roam
lyric poster!

Pathways to Have a Good Roam music:

1.
Scan this QR code
to our web page

2.
Visit queenscarlettproductions.com
and enter the password: ROAMFREE
where prompted on the right side bar.

3.
Music can also be purchased
on CD Baby and iTunes

Another Story Songbook by
Joan Gold Cypress
Illustrated by Lola Buckwald
The Nap Rap
A delightful Rap that's perfect for
putting little ones down to Nap.

Have a Good Roam

A Storybook Song
by Joan Gold Cypress
with Illustrations
by Barbara Counsil

Over the rainbow,
where some gather round
You search for true love,
will it be found?

After a brainstorm,
you'll master the dream
And know that life's
not what it may seem.

Gather your courage
and have a good roam
Just remember,
there's no place like home.

Some days are sunny, happy and bright
Some days are gloomy,
as dark as the night.
It's only weather,
a change will come through
Keep your chin up,
that's what we gotta do.

(Chorus)

The road can narrow be bumpy or wide
Surrender along no matter which side
Look for the magic, see where it goes
Stay focused, the sign ahead shows.

The sky's the limit,
the stars will guide you
Just relax and enjoy the view
Share with your neighbor
and always be kind
Reach out, look up
and see what you'll find.

(Chorus)

Have a good roam.

Joan Gold Cypress, *author*

Joan is a free spirit who makes it a daily practice to be grateful for her family and friends. As a philanthropist, she takes pride in paying it forward, and she loves to share joy with her uplifting, rhyming words.

Joan resides in Eugene, Oregon, a far cry from her Nashville roots. When not writing for her blog or books, she enjoys performing, dancing, gardening and spending time with her family. *Have a Good Roam* is her second children's book. You can order her first book, *The Nap Rap, a rap-along-song* on her website www.queenscarlettproductions.com.

Barbara Counsil, *illustrator*

Barbara grew up among the deciduous forests and rivers of northern Michigan, admiring the drastically changing seasons of colorful trees and heavy snow. She now loves to roam around the mountains of the Pacific Northwest as an art instructor, illustrator, and environmental advocate. Find more of her work at www.marbart.net.

Dawn & Troy Cypress Broadnax, *musicians*

Troy and Dawn Cypress Broadnax have been making music together for more than 20 years. They write and play original music as a duo band, and create children's music for Queen Scarlett Productions. They recently adopted a baby boy and are proud parents with new inspiration for making music for children. Dawn and Troy collaborate in their home studio and look forward to including their child in future creations. You can find their previous musical releases through their website Broadfunk.com.

CPSIA information can be obtained
at www.ICGtesting.com
Printed in the USA
BVHW090119160522
636348BV00002B/11